ENERGY TECHNOLOGY

INSPIRED BY NATURE

by James Bow

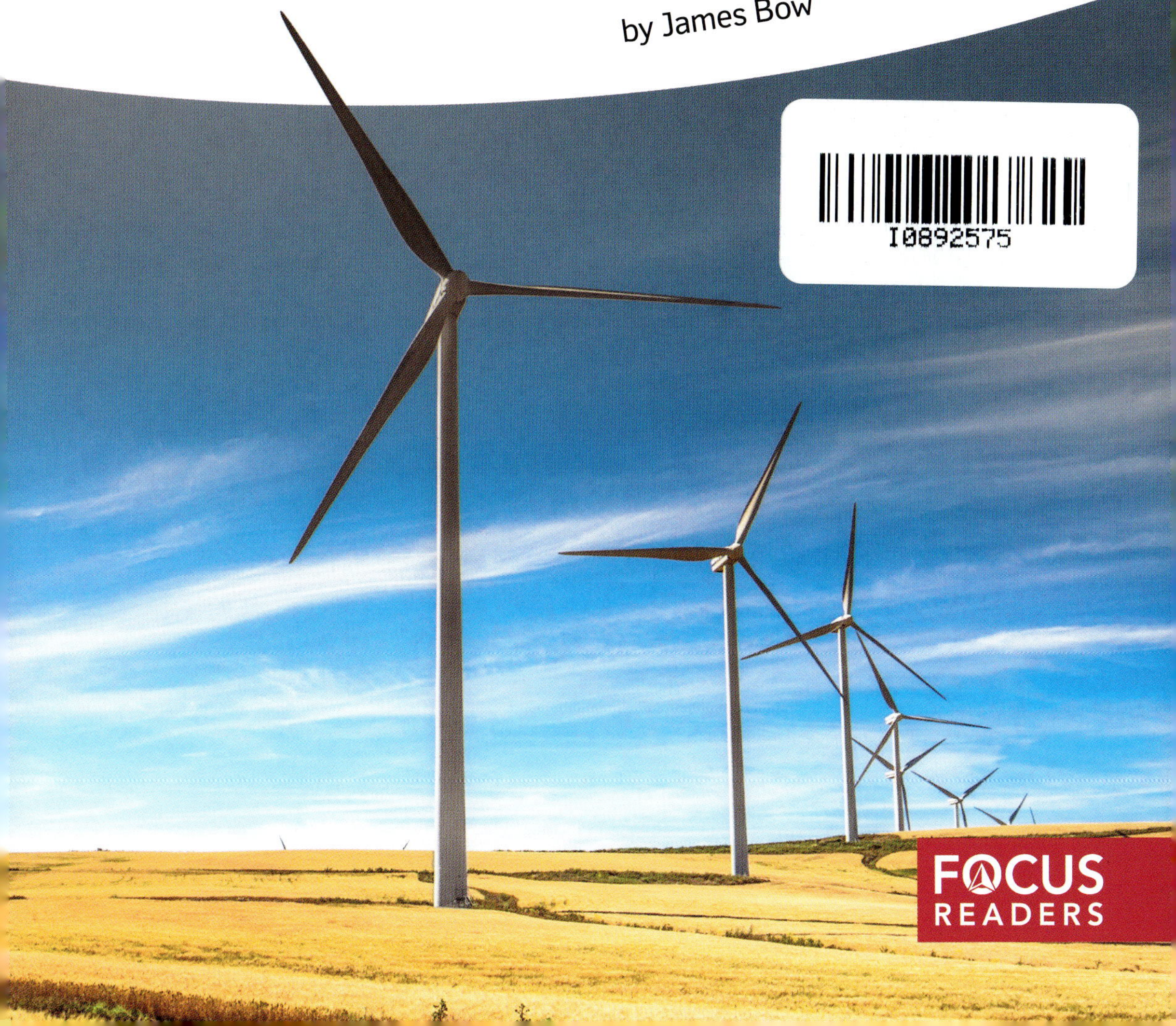

FOCUS READERS

FOCUS READERS

WWW.FOCUSREADERS.COM

Focus Readers is distributed by North Star Editions:
sales@northstareditions.com | 888-417-0195

Produced for Focus Readers by Red Line Editorial.

Content Consultant: Jakki Mohr, PhD, Regents Professor of Marketing, University of Montana

Photographs ©: Lukasz Janyst/Shutterstock Images, cover, 1; AlinaMD/Shutterstock Images, 4–5; ImagineArts/iStockphoto, 7; Felipe Rodriguez/VWPics/AP Images, 8; Jason Isley/Scubazoo/Science Source, 10–11; Laurens Howle/Science Source, 13; Anne Cusack/Los Angeles Times/Getty Images, 15; Kodda/Shutterstock Images, 16–17; Darwin Dale/Science Source, 19; Tesla/UPI/Newscom, 21; Piotr Gatlik/Shutterstock Images, 22–23; Eviart/Shutterstock Images, 24–25; E.R. Degginger/Science Source, 26; ANT Photo Library/Science Source, 29

ISBN
978-1-63517-940-8 (hardcover)
978-1-64185-042-1 (paperback)
978-1-64185-244-9 (ebook pdf)
978-1-64185-143-5 (hosted ebook)

Library of Congress Control Number: 2018932006

Printed in the United States of America
Mankato, MN
May, 2018

ABOUT THE AUTHOR

James Bow is the author of more than 45 nonfiction books for children. He is a graduate of the University of Waterloo in Ontario, Canada, and is a freelance writer and editor. He currently lives outside Toronto, Canada, with his wife and two daughters.

TABLE OF CONTENTS

CHAPTER 1

PLANT POWER

Houses, cars, boats, and buildings all need energy. Without energy, light bulbs would not light up. And cars would not move. In fact, without energy, cars and light bulbs would not even exist.

Scientists are always looking for new energy sources. Some of their best ideas for energy technology come from nature.

Plants gain energy from the sun.

Mimicking nature to solve human problems is called biomimicry.

Plants create the energy they need through **photosynthesis**. In this process, plants absorb sunlight through their leaves. They turn the energy from the sun into energy they can store for later.

Solar panels use a slightly different process. These devices turn sunlight into electricity. Scientists have improved solar panels by studying sunflowers. Sunflowers turn to face the sun during the day. This helps them gather as much energy as possible.

Scientists used a similar method to create a solar **power plant**. They built clusters of mirrors around a central tower. The mirrors reflect the sun's energy at the tower. Then, the tower turns the energy into electricity. Similar to sunflowers, the mirrors turn as the sun crosses the sky.

HOW SOLAR PANELS WORK

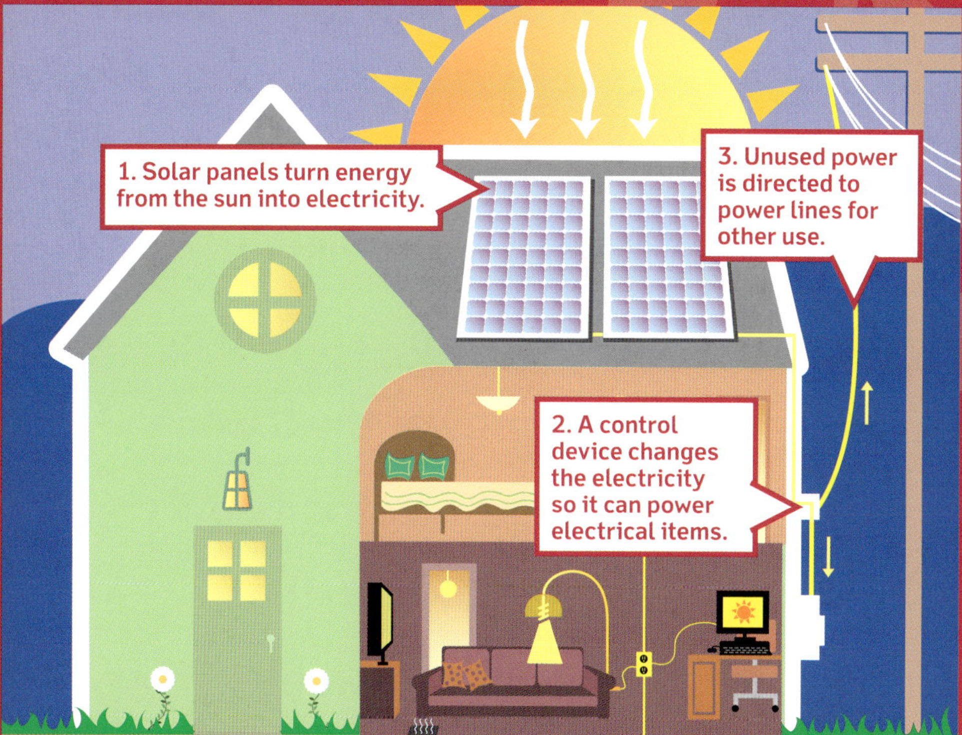

This solar plant in Seville, Spain, has a 40-story tower and 624 mirrors.

But they do not face the sun directly. Instead, the mirrors find an angle that reflects the most energy at the tower.

Humans often create electricity by burning coal and oil. However, these energy sources are not **renewable**. They will eventually run out. Burning coal and oil also releases carbon dioxide into Earth's atmosphere. This process is harmful to the planet. Scientists hope solar power can replace other energy sources.

INSPIRED BY TREES

Windmills turn energy from wind into another form of energy. Scientists have worked to improve windmills by studying trees. They found that branches help trees catch wind. This gave scientists an idea. Most windmills have one large **generator**. But the scientists created a windmill that has many generators. This new windmill has branches, similar to a tree. At the end of each branch is a small generator. Scientists set up the first "tree" windmills in Paris, France, in 2016.

CHAPTER 2

ANIMAL POWER

Many animals have **adapted** to their environments. Their bodies may have features that help them move. For example, whales and dolphins have long, narrow bodies. This shape helps them swim quickly. Some scientists study animals to improve energy technology.

The whale's flippers allow it to steer and propel itself underwater.

They look for ways to produce more power with less effort.

Wind is a major source of renewable energy. But windmills can produce power only when there is a certain amount of wind. Scientists wanted windmills to produce more power. They turned to the humpback whale for answers.

The average humpback weighs more than 80,000 pounds (36,000 kg). It can swim up to 17 miles per hour (27 km/h). Scientists wondered how an animal so big could move so fast. They studied the ridges on the front edge of the humpback's fins. These ridges are called tubercles. They help the whale cut

A scientist displays a model of a humpback flipper. The curved ridges are tubercles.

through water more easily. Scientists added similar ridges to windmill blades. These new windmills can move through the air more easily. That means they make more energy from less wind.

Animals also work together to save energy. For example, geese fly in groups.

They form the shape of a V. The goose in front uses the most energy. As the goose flies, it pushes air upward at the tips of its wings. This upward-moving air helps lift the other geese. As a result, they need less energy to fly.

MIMICKING THE SEA SPONGE

Solar panels are made of an element called silicon. Companies carve and melt silicon to make panels. These methods use large amounts of energy. The sea sponge, a type of sea animal, may have a better idea. Sea sponges create silicon from seawater. They shape the silicon to build their bodies. Scientists hope to mimic how sea sponges grow. The goal is to make silicon form itself into solar panels. This would require less energy than current methods.

Scientists placed windmills in the shape of a diamond.

Fish also move together to save energy. Some schools of fish swim in a diamond shape. Scientists placed windmills in a similar diamond-shaped pattern. The windmill in front created a movement of air. The windmills in back used the movement of air to spin more easily. This helped the windmills make more energy.

CHAPTER 3

SAVING ENERGY

Many energy sources are not renewable. They use up important resources such as oil. They also pollute the air. Humans can protect Earth by using less energy. This is called conservation. Scientists are searching for new ways to conserve energy. They often find solutions in nature.

Coal-powered plants are harmful to the environment.

Fireflies produce a cold light. They waste little energy in the form of heat. To create the light, chemicals react inside the firefly's body. Scientists tried to copy this chemical reaction. But they could not make as much light as the firefly. They studied the firefly closer. They saw that it had small, overlapping scales. The scales help the firefly's light escape outward. This makes the light brighter.

In 2013, scientists applied a similar pattern to light bulbs. They used LEDs, or light-emitting diodes. LEDs use less energy than typical bulbs. The pattern made the LEDs 55 percent brighter. The bulbs used less energy to light a room.

The firefly has a light organ on its abdomen.

Lighting a city is an even greater task. Cities use large power plants to create electricity. One power plant provides electricity to many buildings. However, the electricity must travel far to reach the buildings. As electricity travels, it loses energy in the form of heat. Scientists are looking for other ways to provide power.

Bees may hold the solution. In a beehive, each bee has a small task. But together, the bees build and maintain the hive. Scientists want to mimic this method to power homes and buildings. They would replace one large power plant with many small plants. Homes would have solar panels on the roof.

SHAPED BY STORMS

Tornadoes and whirlpools move in circular patterns. The spiral is a common shape in nature. It allows moving air or water to use less energy to maintain flow. Scientists built fans in a similar circular shape. The fans were able to move air more easily. They used less energy to cool rooms.

The Tesla Powerwall battery (left) stores energy from solar panels.

The energy from the panels would be stored in batteries. Then, the batteries would power nearby homes. That way, the energy would not have to travel far. This could save energy on a large scale.

INSECT INSPIRATION

Termites are skilled builders. They build large, complex mounds in deserts. Despite the hot sun, the mound stays cool. Scientists wondered how this was possible. They found cooler, muddy areas that the termites had built near the bottom of the mounds. Cool air enters the mound from these areas. Inside, warm air rises. It escapes through huge, chimney-like structures.

Termite mounds inspired the design of the Eastgate Centre in Harare, Zimbabwe. The shopping center has shady areas at its base. Inside, hot air rises into large open areas. Then, it escapes through vents in the roof. This design was a success. The Eastgate Centre uses 10 percent of the energy needed to cool similar-sized buildings.

Termite mounds can reach higher than 17 feet (5.2 m).

3:06 PM
86°F

CHAPTER 4

THE FUTURE OF ENERGY

Scientists are still learning how the world works. As they learn more, people will be able to do more using less energy. Nature's blueprints will change the way humans live.

One future technology may be inspired by butterflies. Scientists found that butterfly wings are covered in scales.

In the future, humans may rely more on renewable energy sources.

The morpho butterfly appears blue because of the scales on its wings.

When sunlight hits the wings, the scales reflect the light. This creates shimmering colors. The scales make the wings bright and colorful. Scientists hope to apply similar scales to computer screens. This would allow computers to have brighter screens while using less energy. They would not need a battery to create light.

Batteries are useful sources of energy. But some batteries are large and bulky. They can also die quickly. Scientists want to mimic plants to improve batteries. Plants take in energy from the sun and store it as sugar. They use some of that sugar to create energy. This process inspired scientists to make batteries that are powered by sugar. These would be even lighter and more powerful than the batteries in cellphones.

One scientist is trying to mimic the power of tornadoes. First, the scientist sends hot air into a hollow tower. This creates a small whirlwind. Then, the energy from the whirlwind powers fans.

The fans become generators, creating more energy. The scientist is still trying to make a larger whirlwind. If he does, he could create huge amounts of electricity.

In nature, the parts of an **ecosystem** work together. Plants turn sunlight into energy. Animals eat the plants. Then, the animals' waste helps other plants grow.

Many scientists think cities should act like ecosystems. Different parts of the city could work together to save energy. For example, one company in California uses waste from power plants to make cement. The waste contains carbon dioxide gas. The company turns the gas into **calcium carbonate**. This

Coral reefs are made up of layers of calcium carbonate.

mineral is an ingredient in cement. Sea animals also use a form of the mineral to build shells and reefs.

Usually, making cement requires large amounts of energy. But the California company saves energy by using another industry's waste. By following this company's example, ecosystem-inspired cities could grow using less energy.

FOCUS ON

ENERGY TECHNOLOGY INSPIRED BY NATURE

Write your answers on a separate piece of paper.

1. Write a summary of one of the technologies featured in Chapter 1.
2. Which energy-inspired technologies would you want in your home? Why?
3. What is an example of a non-renewable energy source?
   - A. sunlight
   - B. wind
   - C. coal
4. What would happen if fireflies did not have scales?
   - A. Their light would be brighter.
   - B. Their light would be less bright.
   - C. They would not be able to create light.

Answer key on page 32.

GLOSSARY

adapted
Changed over time to deal with a certain situation.

calcium carbonate
A solid substance found in nature as chalk, limestone, and marble.

ecosystem
The collection of living things in a natural area.

generator
A machine that produces electricity.

mimicking
Copying an appearance or behavior.

photosynthesis
The process in which plants turn sunlight, carbon dioxide, and water into oxygen and energy.

power plant
A place that generates electricity.

renewable
Having to do with natural resources that never run out.

solar
Having to do with the sun.

TO LEARN MORE

BOOKS

Doeden, Matt. *Finding Out about Wind Energy.* Minneapolis: Lerner Publications, 2015.

Green, Dan. *Eyewitness Energy.* New York: DK Publishing, 2016.

Yomtov, Nel. *From Termite Den to . . . Office Building.* Ann Arbor, MI: Cherry Lake Publishing, 2014.

NOTE TO EDUCATORS

Visit **www.focusreaders.com** to find lesson plans, activities, links, and other resources related to this title.

INDEX

Answer Key: 1. Answers will vary; **2.** Answers will vary; **3.** C; **4.** B